For my children
with love and hope
D. G.

First published in Great Britain in 2008 by Bloomsbury Publishing Plc.
Published in the United States of America in 2008 by Walker Publishing Company, Inc.

For information about permission to reproduce selections from this book, write to Permissions,
Walker & Company, 175 Fifth Avenue, New York, New York 10010

Library of Congress Cataloging-in-Publication Data
Gliori, Debi.
The trouble with dragons / by Debi Gliori. — 1st ed.
p.   cm.
Summary: When dragons cut down too many trees, blow out too much hot air,
and do other environmental damage, the future looks grim, but other animals
advise them on how to mend their ways and save the planet.
ISBN-13: 978-0-8027-9789-6 · ISBN-10: 0-8027-9789-X (hardcover)
ISBN-13: 978-0-8027-9790-2 · ISBN-10: 0-8027-9790-3 (reinforced)
[1. Stories in rhyme. 2. Conservation of natural resources—Fiction.
3. Environmental protection—Fiction. 4. Dragons—Fiction.] I. Title.
PZ8.3.G47Tro 2008   [E]—dc22   2008005389

The illustrations in this book were created using watercolor
Typeset in St Nicholas

Visit Walker & Company's Web site at www.walkeryoungreaders.com

Printed in Belgium by Proost
2 4 6 8 10 9 7 5 3 1 (hardcover)
2 4 6 8 10 9 7 5 3 1 (reinforced)

FSC
Mixed Sources
Product group from well-managed
forests and recycled wood or fibre
Cert no. BV-COC-070303
www.fsc.org
© 1996 Forest Stewardship Council

The Trouble with Dragons

Debi Gliori

Walker & Company · New York

The trouble with dragons is . . .
dragons make dragons
and then they make more
till there's wall-to-wall dragons
making dragons galore.

Then dragons start spreading all over the place.

Soon their houses and roads take up all of the space.

Dragons eat all the food and drink all the drink
and use everything up without stopping to think.
They also throw parties and make lots of noise
and leave a huge mess after playing with their toys.

Dragons chop down the forests,
which melts both the poles
and punctures the atmosphere
full of big holes.

Dragons blow out hot air,

which makes everything hotter . . .

and hotter . . .

and hotter . . .

until all the snow melts

and the ice turns to water.

Then the seas start to rise
and the deserts expand
until everything's covered
in water
or sand.

Say good-bye to the world
into which you were born,
for the dragons have made it
all tattered and torn.

Poor dragons.

Imagine a world with no birds and no bees—
just dragons as far as a dragon can see.
"Don't go," wailed the dragons. "Don't leave us alone.
A world without wildlife is no kind of home."

"If you stay, we all promise
to do what it takes

to look after the planet
for all of our sakes."

As the waters rose higher,
right over their knees,

a voice said, "Okay, start by *not*
chopping down trees."

Then all of the animals
chimed in with advice.

From the greatest of elephants

to the smallest of mice.

"Eat food
that is grown
much closer to home,

and
leave
the wild places
and
ice caps

alone."

"Turn down your heaters and get some fresh air.

There's enough to go round if we all share."

"Respect all Earth's creatures
and cherish the land.
Recycle, reuse, and reduce
your demands."

So . . . if you know a dragon
(and most of us do),
ask if it thinks
that this story is true.

For if we can't see that
our stories are linked,
then sadly,
like dragons,
we could be
extinct.